THE GREAT GRACIE CHASE
STOP THAT DOG!

By Cynthia Rylant

Illustrated by Mark Teague

SCHOLASTIC INC.
New York Toronto London Auckland Sydney
Mexico City New Delhi Hong Kong Buenos Aires

This book was originally published in hardcover by the Blue Sky Press in 2001.

ISBN 0-590-10044-0

Text copyright © 2001 by Cynthia Rylant
Illustrations copyright © 2001 by Mark Teague
All rights reserved.
Published by Scholastic Inc. SCHOLASTIC and associated logos are trademarks and/or registered trademarks of Scholastic Inc.

12 11 10 9 8 7 6 5 4 3 2 1   2 3 4 5 6 7/0
Printed in the U.S.A.   08
First Scholastic paperback printing, January 2002

Once there was a little round dog named
Gracie Rose. She was a very good dog.
She helped the bigger dog watch the house.
She kept the kitty company.
She even sang to the fish
when it was lonely.

You see, Gracie loved a *quiet* house. She loved the kitty sleeping on the windowsill, the big dog sleeping on the couch, the quiet fish going *ploop-ploop*. For Gracie, a quiet home was the best home.

Gracie Rose was good every single day of her life— except for one . . . the day the painters came.

Gracie did not like painters, but she did not know this until the day they came to her house.

So, when they arrived one day to paint Gracie's kitchen, she did not like it! Here they came in a big, noisy truck!

BOB'S PAINTING
"WE DO OUR BEST"

There they were at the door with their clangy ladders and big-person voices! There they were, dragging chairs across Gracie's quiet kitchen floor! Gracie Rose watched them with her ears straight up in the air and she was not happy. She barked and barked and told them to go outside. But do you know what?

Gracie was put outside!

And she did not like it *one bit*!

So Gracie, that silly little dog who loved a quiet house, decided to do something naughty. Gracie decided to take a walk— ALL BY HERSELF!

Someone had left the gate open. Probably a busy painter. Gracie was supposed to be a good dog and never go through that gate by herself.

But she did! And when she was halfway down the street, she heard someone say loudly, "WHERE'S GRACIE?"

And that began the Great Gracie Chase.

Because when the people in the house came outside to find her, and the painters came outside, and the neighbors came outside, and the garbage man stepped out of his truck, and the paperboy stopped his bike, and the delivery woman pulled over, and everyone said, *"THERE'S GRACIE!"* Gracie started to run!

BIG ED'S SANITATION

Gracie did not know why she was running except that suddenly everybody in the world was trying to catch her! And she did not want to be caught! So Gracie ran down the street and everybody else ran down the street, too.

Gracie ran up the hill and everybody else ran up the hill.

Gracie ran across the schoolyard and everybody else
ran across the schoolyard.

Gracie ran through the water fountain and everybody
else ran through the water fountain. (Well, except
the cat, who did not like water fountains.)

The chase got bigger. "Stop that dog!" everybody cried, which only made Gracie run faster. And soon the whole town was watching (or running in) the Great Gracie Chase!

Poor little Gracie. She did not like this walk
ALL BY HERSELF. It was too quick and too noisy
and all she wanted was to be beside her fish again.
But she couldn't stop running now!
Everyone wanted to catch her!

So she ran. And ran. And ran. Until pretty soon the painters had to stop because they couldn't catch their breath. And the delivery woman had to stop because her feet hurt. And the paperboy had to stop because his bike broke. And someone else had to stop because she tripped and fell. And one by one by one, all the people had to stop BECAUSE THEY COULD NOT KEEP UP WITH GRACIE!

Then suddenly Gracie realized how *quiet* everything was again.

She looked behind her, and the whole world was quiet.

People were resting. How nice, Gracie thought.

So that silly little dog turned around and walked back home ALL BY HERSELF!

The painters did not return to Gracie's house that day. They had to go take naps.

And once again,

Gracie had a quiet home.

She was happy.

That silly little dog!